Dust Bunny Dance

Words by
Susie Sivill

Pictures by
Chord LeClaire

Dust Bunny Dance

Susie Sivill

Illustrated by Chord LeClaire

Dust Bunny Publishing

La Crosse, Wisconsin

Published by: Bookmarketeers.com
ISBN No: 978-1-0880-3917-5

dust bunny

/dəst 'bənē/

noun
A ball of dust or fluff that is sometimes found under your couch or bed. It lives there because busy families would rather spend their time playing and reading together instead of cleaning.

I hope the dust bunnies in your life remind you that you are loved.

To my family:
Mark, Anna, Michael, Alex and Travis.
Thanks for believing in me.

yed with my grandma for the first time last night.

tucked me in Momma's old bed, way too tight.

ed to sound brave, but my voice squeaked instead

en I asked, "would you take a look under the

?"

"Now Elenore Jo" she quickly remarked.

"I would never let monsters stay here in the dark.

But if worries and fears make your mind start to wonder, I will

take a quick look to see what's down under."

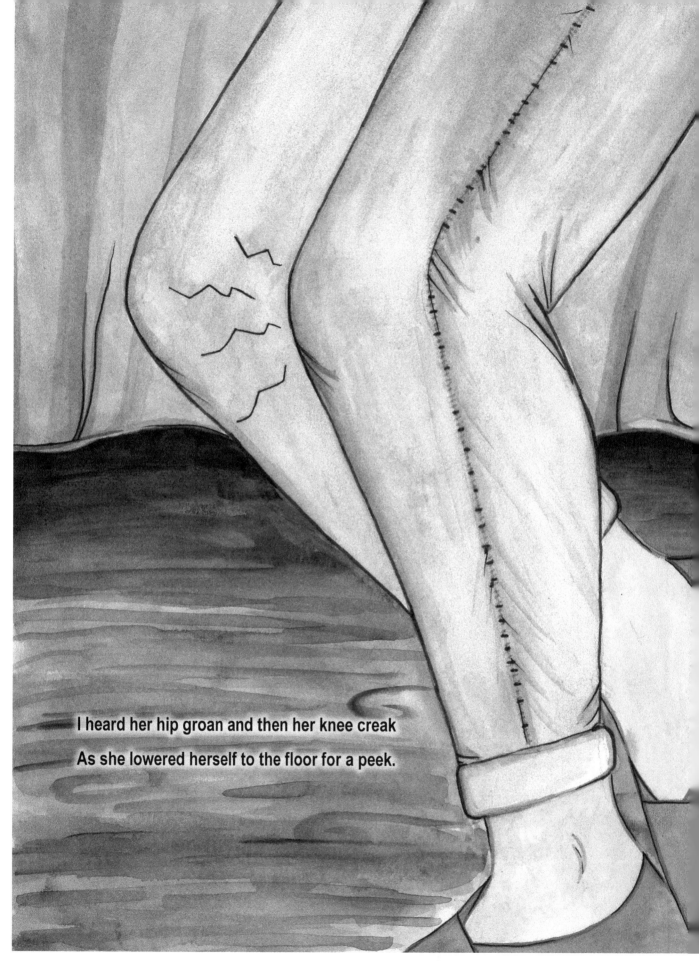

I heard her hip groan and then her knee creak

As she lowered herself to the floor for a peek.

When she pulled back the sheet, she gasped in surprise

Then slowly stood up wiping tears from her eyes.

When I peeked, two big eyes stared at me from the floor.
And then four and then six and then eight and then more!
"What are they?" I asked. "Are they zombies or ghosts?
Will they nibble my fingers or bite at my toes?"

"They are dust bunnies," she sighed,

"lots of dust bunnies, dear,

They come to my house

at this time every year.

I will go get a broom

and will sweep them away.

That dust makes me sneeze!

It just cannot stay!"

As she went for her broom I said, "Please, that's not right.

Those dust bunnies might make good friends ... they just might.

I think we should first get to know them instead."

Then, I took a big jump and leapt out of bed.

As my feet hit the floor, from out of the gloom
A single dust bunny rolled into the room.
He winked his left eye and gave me a smile
As if to say "Can't we just play for a while?"

ould see in an instant that we could have fun.
mped up on my feet and started to run.
I dashed past my bed with a zip and a zoom
re dust bunnies skated out into the room!

I ran for the window and opened it wide
And asked the north wind to come meet us inside.
Then I turned on the fan and they all came alive
They were buzzing like bees who are leaving the hive

From out of the corners, the dark nooks and crannies
Came the dust bunny grandpas and dust bunny grannies.
The cousins and babies and uncles and aunts.
They made a big circle holding each other's hands.

"IT'S TIME" they all cried, "F

They started out slow, pairing up two by two

And waltzed like I once saw my grandparents do.

Then they all speeded up, dancing disco and sw

While some did a rock and roll any old thi

The square dancers all did a sharp do-si-do

While the chorus girl bunnies lined up in a row.

The dust ballerina jumped onto the desk

And treated us all to a quick arabesque.

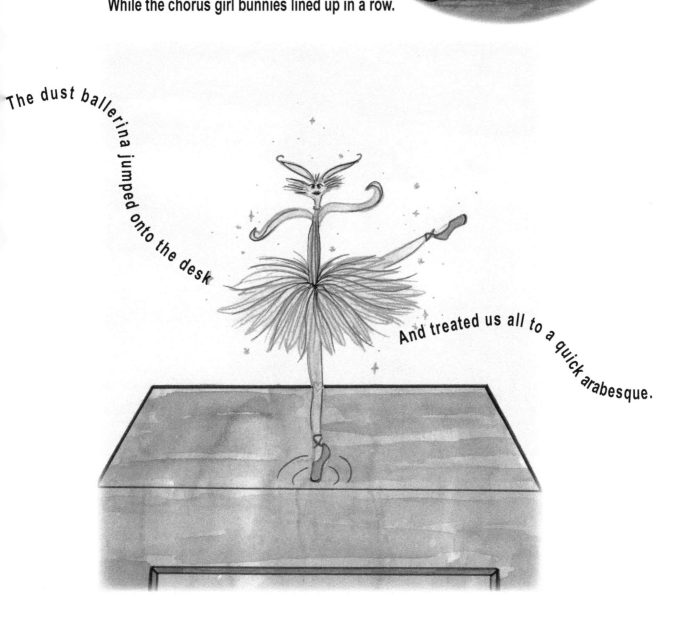

As the dancing grew faster, the dust bunnies flew.

They line danced and tap danced and bunny hopped too.

And as the break dancers spun into the room . . .

"This dancing must stop!" she said with a wheeze.

"I'm begging you,
please make them stop,
will you please?"

Her hair was a tangle on top of her head.

Her pretty blue eyes had turned puffy and red.

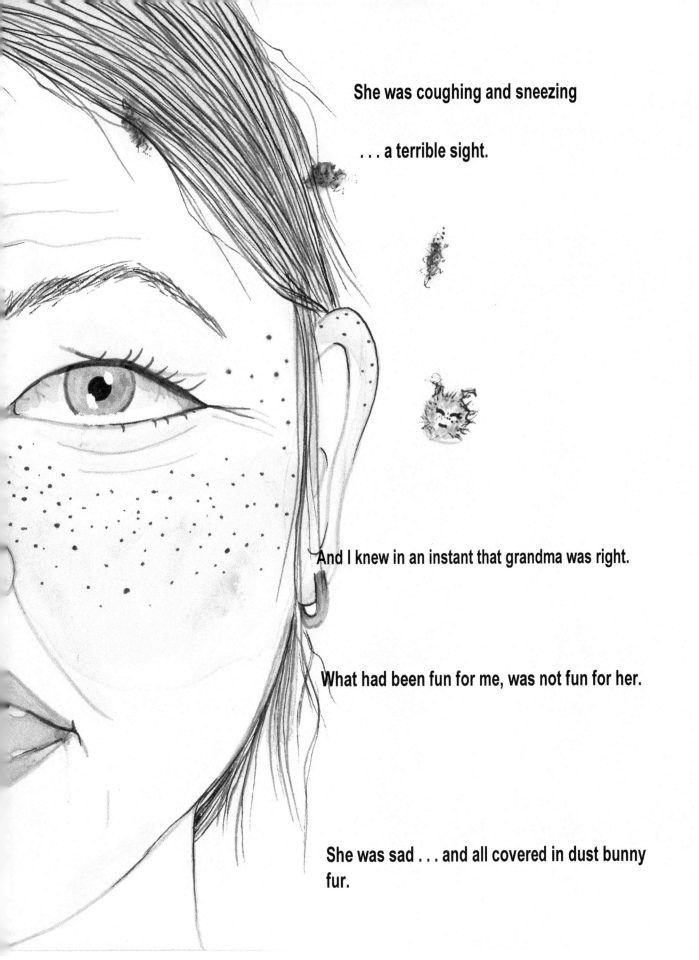

She was coughing and sneezing

. . . a terrible sight.

And I knew in an instant that grandma was right.

What had been fun for me, was not fun for her.

She was sad . . . and all covered in dust bunny fur.

So I pulled down the window and turned off the fan. The dancing dust bunnies all started to land. They looked at me sadly, but all seemed to know That the dancing was over. It was now time to go.

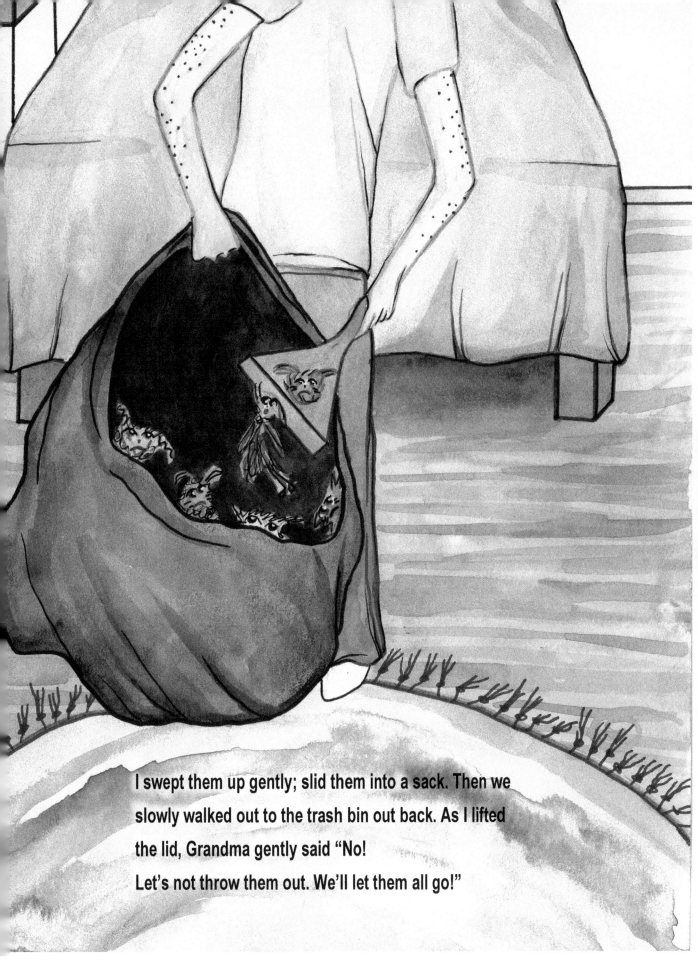

I swept them up gently; slid them into a sack. Then we
slowly walked out to the trash bin out back. As I lifted
the lid, Grandma gently said "No!
Let's not throw them out. We'll let them all go!"

We carefully poured them out into a heap
And watched as the wind woke them up from
their sleep.

A C H O O !

As my Grandma let loose with one final

A C H O O !

into the air, all the dust bunnies flew!

As the dust bunnies danced away into the sky

We cheered and we waved them a final goodbye.

See you next year . . .

CPSIA information can be obtained
at www.ICGtesting.com
Printed in the USA
LVHW071756201122
733506LV00008B/182